George
Kranky

Mr Killy
Kranky

Mrs
Kranky

Grandma

ROALD DAHL

GEORGE'S
Marvellous Medicine

ILLUSTRATED BY QUENTIN BLAKE

PUFFIN

Find out more about Roald Dahl
by visiting the website at
roalddahl.com

PUFFIN BOOKS

Published by the Penguin Group
Penguin Books Ltd, 80 Strand, London WC2R ORL, England
Penguin Group (USA) Inc., 375 Hudson Street, New York, New York 10014, USA
Penguin Group (Canada), 90 Eglinton Avenue East, Suite 700, Toronto, Ontario, Canada M4P 2Y3
(a division of Pearson Penguin Canada Inc.)
Penguin Ireland, 25 St Stephen's Green, Dublin 2, Ireland (a division of Penguin Books Ltd)
Penguin Group (Australia), 707 Collins Street, Melbourne, Victoria 3008, Australia
(a division of Pearson Australia Group Pty Ltd)
Penguin Books India Pvt Ltd, 11 Community Centre, Panchsheel Park, New Delhi – 110 017, India
Penguin Group (NZ), 67 Apollo Drive, Rosedale, Auckland 0632, New Zealand
(a division of Pearson New Zealand Ltd)
Penguin Books (South Africa) (Pty) Ltd, Block D, Rosebank Office Park, 181 Jan Smuts Avenue,
Parktown North, Gauteng 2193, South Africa

Penguin Books Ltd, Registered Offices: 80 Strand, London WC2R ORL, England

puffinbooks.com

First published in Great Britain by Jonathan Cape 1981
Published in Puffin Books 1982
This edition published 2013
007

Text copyright © Roald Dahl Nominee Ltd, 1981
Illustrations copyright © Quentin Blake, 1981
The moral right of the author and illustrator has been asserted
All rights reserved

Set in Monotype Baskerville
Printed in Great Britain by Clays Ltd, St Ives plc

Except in the United States of America, this book is sold subject to the condition that it shall not, by way of
trade or otherwise, be lent, re-sold, hired out, or otherwise circulated without the publisher's prior consent in any
form of binding or cover other than that in which it is published and without a similar condition including this
condition being imposed on the subsequent purchaser

British Library Cataloguing in Publication Data
A CIP catalogue record for this book is available from the British Library

ISBN: 978-0-141-34992-3

www.greenpenguin.co.uk

MIX
Paper from
responsible sources
FSC
www.fsc.org   FSC® C018179

Penguin Books is committed to a sustainable
future for our business, our readers and our planet.
This book is made from Forest Stewardship
Council™ certified paper.

Contents

Grandma

'I'm going shopping in the village,' George's mother said to George on Saturday morning. 'So be a good boy and don't get up to mischief.'

This was a silly thing to say to a small boy at any time. It immediately made him wonder what sort of mischief he might get up to.

'And don't forget to give Grandma her medicine at eleven o'clock,' the mother said. Then out she went, closing the back door behind her.

Grandma, who was dozing in her chair by the window, opened one wicked little eye and said, 'Now you heard what your mother said, George. Don't forget my medicine.'

'No, Grandma,' George said.

'And just try to behave yourself for once while she's away.'

'Yes, Grandma,' George said.

George was bored to tears. He didn't have a brother or a sister. His father was a farmer and the farm they lived on was miles away from any-where, so there were never any children to play with. He was tired of staring at pigs and hens and cows and sheep. He was especially tired of having to live in the same house as that grizzly old grunion of a Grandma. Looking after her all by himself was hardly the most exciting way to spend a Saturday morning.

'You can make me a nice cup of tea for a start,' Grandma said to George. 'That'll keep you out of mischief for a few minutes.'

'Yes, Grandma,' George said.

George couldn't help disliking Grandma. She was a selfish grumpy old woman. She had pale brown teeth and a small puckered-up mouth like a dog's bottom.

'How much sugar in your tea today, Grandma?' George asked her.

'One spoon,' she said. 'And no milk.'

Most grandmothers are lovely, kind, helpful old ladies, but not this one. She spent all day and every day sitting in her chair by the window, and she was always complaining, grousing, grouching, grumbling, griping about something or other. Never once, even on her best days, had she smiled at George and said, 'Well, how are you this morning, George?' or 'Why don't you and I have a game of Snakes and Ladders?' or 'How was school today?' She didn't seem to care about other people, only about herself. She was a miserable old grouch.

George went into the kitchen and made
Grandma a cup of tea with a teabag. He put one
spoon of sugar in it and no milk. He stirred the
sugar well and carried the cup into the living-
room.

Grandma sipped the tea. 'It's not sweet
enough,' she said. 'Put more sugar in.'

George took the cup back to the kitchen and
added another spoonful of sugar. He stirred it
again and carried it carefully in to Grandma.

'Where's the saucer?' she said. 'I won't have a
cup without a saucer.'

George fetched her a saucer.

'And what about a teaspoon, if you please?'

'I've stirred it for you, Grandma. I stirred it well.'

'I'll stir my own tea, thank you very much,' she said. 'Fetch me a teaspoon.'

George fetched her a teaspoon.

When George's mother or father were home, Grandma never ordered George about like this. It was only when she had him on her own that she began treating him badly.

'You know what's the matter with you?' the old woman said, staring at George over the rim of the teacup with those bright wicked little eyes. 'You're *growing* too fast. Boys who grow too fast become stupid and lazy.'

'But I can't help it if I'm growing fast, Grandma,' George said.

'Of course you can,' she snapped. 'Growing's a nasty childish habit.'

'But we *have* to grow, Grandma. If we didn't grow, we'd never be grown-ups.'

'Rubbish, boy, rubbish,' she said. 'Look at me. Am I growing? Certainly not.'

'But you did once, Grandma.'

'Only *very little*,' the old woman answered. 'I gave up growing when I was extremely small, along with all the other nasty childish habits like

4

laziness and disobedience and greed and sloppiness and untidiness and stupidity. You haven't given up any of these things, have you?'

'I'm still only a little boy, Grandma.'

'You're eight years old,' she snorted. 'That's old enough to know better. If you don't stop growing soon, it'll be too late.'

'Too late for what, Grandma?'

'It's ridiculous,' she went on. 'You're nearly as tall as me already.'

George took a good look at Grandma. She certainly was a *very tiny* person. Her legs were so short she had to have a footstool to put her feet on, and her head only came halfway up the back of the armchair.

'Daddy says it's fine for a man to be tall,' George said.

'Don't listen to your daddy,' Grandma said. 'Listen to me.'

'But how do I stop myself growing?' George asked her.

'Eat less chocolate,' Grandma said.

'Does chocolate make you grow?'

'It makes you grow the *wrong way*,' she snapped. 'Up instead of down.'

Grandma sipped some tea but never took her eyes from the little boy who stood before her.

'Never grow up,' she said. 'Always down.'

'Yes, Grandma.'

'And stop eating chocolate. Eat cabbage instead.'

'Cabbage! Oh no, I don't like cabbage,' George said.

'It's not what you like or what you don't like,' Grandma snapped. 'It's what's good for you that counts. From now on, you must eat cabbage three times a day. Mountains of cabbage! And if it's got caterpillars in it, so much the better!'

'Owch,' George said.

'Caterpillars give you brains,' the old woman said.

'Mummy washes them down the sink,' George said.

'Mummy's as stupid as you are,' Grandma said. 'Cabbage doesn't taste of anything without a few boiled caterpillars in it. Slugs, too.'

'Not *slugs*!' George cried out. 'I couldn't eat slugs!'

'Whenever I see a live slug on a piece of lettuce,' Grandma said, 'I gobble it up quick before it crawls away. Delicious.' She squeezed her lips together tight so that her mouth became a tiny wrinkled hole. 'Delicious,' she said again. 'Worms and slugs and beetley bugs. You don't know what's good for you.'

'You're joking, Grandma.'

'I never joke,' she said. 'Beetles are perhaps best of all. They go *crunch*!'

'Grandma! That's beastly!'

The old hag grinned, showing those pale brown teeth. 'Sometimes, if you're lucky,' she said, 'you get a beetle inside the stem of a stick of celery. That's what I like.'

'Grandma! How *could* you?'

'You find all sorts of nice things in sticks of raw celery,' the old woman went on. 'Sometimes it's earwigs.'

'I don't want to hear about it!' cried George.

'A big fat earwig is very tasty,' Grandma said, licking her lips. 'But you've got to be very quick, my dear, when you put one of those in your mouth. It has a pair of sharp nippers on its back end and if it grabs your tongue with those, it never lets go. So you've got to bite the earwig first, *chop chop*, before it bites you.'

George started edging towards the door. He wanted to get as far away as possible from this filthy old woman.

'You're trying to get away from me, aren't you?' she said, pointing a finger straight at George's face. 'You're trying to get away from Grandma.'

Little George stood by the door staring at the old hag in the chair. She stared back at him.

Could it be, George wondered, that she was a witch? He had always thought witches were only in fairy tales, but now he was not so sure.

'Come closer to me, little boy,' she said, beckoning to him with a horny finger. 'Come closer to me and I will tell you *secrets*.'

George didn't move.

Grandma didn't move either.

'I know a great many secrets,' she said, and suddenly she smiled. It was a thin icy smile, the kind a snake might make just before it bites you. 'Come over here to Grandma and she'll whisper secrets to you.'

George took a step backwards, edging closer to the door.

'You mustn't be frightened of your old Grandma,' she said, smiling that icy smile.

George took another step backwards.

'Some of us,' she said, and all at once she was leaning forward in her chair and whispering in a throaty sort of voice George had never heard her use before. 'Some of us,' she said, 'have magic powers that can twist the creatures of this earth into wondrous shapes . . .'

A tingle of electricity flashed down the length of George's spine. He began to feel frightened.

'Some of us,' the old woman went on, 'have fire on our tongues and sparks in our bellies and wizardry in the tips of our fingers . . .

'Some of us know secrets that would make your hair stand straight up on end and your eyes pop out of their sockets . . .'

George wanted to run away, but his feet seemed stuck to the floor.

'We know how to make your nails drop off and teeth grow out of your fingers instead.'

George began to tremble. It was her face that frightened him most of all, the frosty smile, the brilliant unblinking eyes.

'We know how to have you wake up in the morning with a long tail coming out from behind you.'

'Grandma!' he cried out. 'Stop!'

'We know secrets, my dear, about dark places where dark things live and squirm and slither all over each other . . .'

George made a dive for the door.

'It doesn't matter how far you run,' he heard her saying, 'you won't ever get away . . .'

George ran into the kitchen, slamming the door behind him.

The Marvellous Plan

George sat himself down at the table in the kitchen. He was shaking a little. Oh, how he hated Grandma! He really *hated* that horrid old witchy woman. And all of a sudden he had a tremendous urge to *do something* about her. Something *whopping*. Something *absolutely terrific*. A *real shocker*. A sort of explosion. He wanted to blow away the witchy smell that hung about her in the next room. He may have been only eight years old but he was a brave little boy. He was ready to take this old woman on.

'I'm not going to be frightened by *her*,' he said softly to himself. But he *was* frightened. And that's why he wanted suddenly to explode her away.

Well . . . not quite away. But he did want to shake the old woman up a bit.

Very well, then. What should it be, this whopping terrific exploding shocker for Grandma?

He would have liked to put a firework banger under her chair but he didn't have one.

He would have liked to put a long green snake down the back of her dress but he didn't have a long green snake.

He would have liked to put six big black rats in the room with her and lock the door but he didn't have six big black rats.

As George sat there pondering this interesting problem, his eye fell upon the bottle of Grandma's brown medicine standing on the sideboard. Rotten stuff it seemed to be. Four times a day a large spoonful of it was shovelled into her mouth and it didn't do her the slightest bit of good. She was always just as horrid after she'd had it as she'd been before. The whole point of medicine, surely, was to make a person better. If it didn't do that, then it was quite useless.

So-ho! thought George suddenly. *Ah-ha! Ho-hum!* I know exactly what I'll do. I shall make her a *new* medicine, one that is so strong and so fierce and so fantastic it will either cure her completely or blow off the top of her head. I'll make her a *magic medicine*, a medicine no doctor in the world has ever made before.

George looked at the kitchen clock. It said five past ten. There was nearly an hour left before Grandma's next dose was due at eleven.

'Here we go, then!' cried George, jumping up from the table. 'A magic medicine it shall be!'

'So give me a bug and a jumping flea,
Give me two snails and lizards three,
And a slimy squiggler from the sea,
And the poisonous sting of a bumblebee,
And the juice from the fruit of the ju-jube tree,
And the powdered bone of a wombat's knee.
And one hundred other things as well
Each with a rather nasty smell.
I'll stir them up, I'll boil them long,
A mixture tough, a mixture strong.
And then, heigh-ho, and down it goes,
A nice big spoonful (hold your nose)
Just gulp it down and have no fear.
"How do you like it, Granny dear?"

Will she go pop? Will she explode?
Will she go flying down the road?
Will she go poof in a puff of smoke?
Start fizzing like a can of Coke?
Who knows? Not I. Let's wait and see.
(I'm glad it's neither you nor me.)
Oh Grandma, if you only knew
What I have got in store for you!'

George Begins to Make the Medicine

George took an enormous saucepan out of the cupboard and placed it on the kitchen table.

'George!' came the shrill voice from the next room. 'What are you doing?'

'Nothing, Grandma,' he called out.

'You needn't think I can't hear you just because you closed the door! You're rattling the saucepans!'

'I'm just tidying the kitchen, Grandma.'

Then there was silence.

George had absolutely no doubts whatsoever about how he was going to make his famous medicine. He wasn't going to fool about wondering whether to put in a little bit of this or a little bit of that. Quite simply, he was going to put in EVERYTHING he could find. There would be no messing about, no hesitating, no wondering whether a particular thing would knock the old girl sideways or not. The rule would be this: whatever he saw, if it was runny or powdery or gooey, in it went.

Nobody had ever made a medicine like that before. If it didn't actually cure Grandma, then it would anyway cause some exciting results. It would be worth watching.

George decided to work his way round the various rooms one at a time and see what they had to offer.

He would go first to the bathroom. There are always lots of funny things in a bathroom. So upstairs he went, carrying the enormous two-handled saucepan before him.

In the bathroom, he gazed longingly at the famous and dreaded medicine cupboard. But he didn't go near it. It was the only thing in the entire house he was forbidden to touch. He had made solemn promises to his parents about this and he wasn't going to break them. There were things in there, they had told him, that could actually kill a person, and although he was out to give Grandma a pretty fiery mouthful, he didn't really want a dead body on his hands. George put the saucepan on the floor and went to work.

Number one was a bottle labelled GOLDEN GLOSS HAIR SHAMPOO. He emptied it into the pan. 'That ought to wash her tummy nice and clean,' he said.

He took a full tube of TOOTHPASTE and squeezed out the whole lot of it in one long worm. 'Maybe that will brighten up those horrid brown teeth of hers,' he said.

There was an aerosol can of SUPERFOAM SHAVING SOAP belonging to his father. George loved playing with aerosols. He pressed the button and kept his finger on it until there was nothing left. A wonderful mountain of white foam built up in the giant saucepan.

With his fingers, he scooped out the contents of a jar of VITAMIN ENRICHED FACE CREAM.

In went a small bottle of scarlet NAIL VARNISH. 'If the toothpaste doesn't clean her teeth,' George said, 'then this will paint them as red as roses.'

He found another jar of creamy stuff labelled HAIR REMOVER. SMEAR IT ON YOUR LEGS, it said, AND ALLOW TO REMAIN FOR FIVE MINUTES. George tipped it all into the saucepan.

There was a bottle with yellow stuff inside it called DISHWORTH'S FAMOUS DANDRUFF CURE. In it went.

There was something called BRILLIDENT FOR CLEANING FALSE TEETH. It was a white powder. In that went, too.

He found another aerosol can, NEVERMORE PONKING DEODORANT SPRAY, GUARANTEED, it said, TO KEEP AWAY UNPLEASANT BODY SMELLS FOR A WHOLE DAY. 'She could use plenty of that,' George said as he sprayed the entire canful into the saucepan.

LIQUID PARAFFIN, the next one was called. It was a big bottle. He hadn't the faintest idea what it did to you, but he poured it in anyway.

That, he thought, looking around him, was about all from the bathroom.

On his mother's dressing-table in the bedroom, George found yet another lovely aerosol can. It was called HELGA'S HAIRSET. HOLD TWELVE INCHES AWAY FROM THE HAIR AND SPRAY LIGHTLY. He squirted the whole lot into the saucepan. He *did* enjoy squirting these aerosols.

There was a bottle of perfume called FLOWERS OF TURNIPS. It smelled of old cheese. In it went.

And in, too, went a large round box of POWDER. It was called PINK PLASTER. There was a powder-puff on top and he threw that in as well for luck.

He found a couple of LIPSTICKS. He pulled

the greasy red things out of their little cases and added them to the mixture.

The bedroom had nothing more to offer, so George carried the enormous saucepan downstairs again and trotted into the laundry-room where the shelves were full of all kinds of household items.

The first one he took down was a large box of SUPERWHITE FOR AUTOMATIC WASHING-MACHINES. DIRT, it said, WILL DISAPPEAR LIKE MAGIC. George didn't know whether Grandma was automatic or not, but she was certainly a dirty old woman. 'So she'd better have it all,' he said, tipping in the whole boxful.

Then there was a big tin of WAXWELL FLOOR POLISH. IT REMOVES FILTH AND FOUL MESSES FROM YOUR FLOOR AND LEAVES EVERYTHING SHINY BRIGHT, it said. George scooped the orange-coloured waxy stuff out of the tin and plonked it into the pan.

There was a round cardboard carton labelled FLEA POWDER FOR DOGS. KEEP WELL AWAY FROM THE DOG'S FOOD, it said,
BECAUSE THIS
POWDER, IF
EATEN, WILL
MAKE THE DOG

EXPLODE. 'Good,' said George, pouring it all into the saucepan.

He found a box of CANARY SEED on the shelf. 'Perhaps it'll make the old bird sing,' he said, and in it went.

Next, George explored the box with shoe-cleaning materials – brushes and tins and dusters. Well now, he thought, Grandma's medicine is brown, so *my* medicine must also be brown or she'll smell a rat. The way to colour it, he decided, would be with BROWN SHOE-POLISH. The large tin he chose was labelled DARK TAN. Splendid. He scooped it all out with an old spoon and plopped it into the pan. He would stir it up later.

On his way back to the kitchen, George saw a bottle of GIN standing on the sideboard. Grandma was very fond of gin. She was allowed to have a small nip of it every evening. Now he would give her a treat. He would pour in the whole bottle. He did.

Back in the kitchen, George put the huge

saucepan on the table and went over to the cupboard that served as a larder. The shelves were bulging with bottles and jars of every sort. He chose the following and emptied them one by one into the saucepan:

A TIN OF CURRY POWDER

A TIN OF MUSTARD POWDER

A BOTTLE OF 'EXTRA HOT' CHILLI SAUCE

A TIN OF BLACK PEPPERCORNS

A BOTTLE OF HORSERADISH SAUCE

'There!' he said aloud. 'That should do it!'

'George!' came the screechy voice from the next room. 'Who are you talking to in there? What are you up to?'

'Nothing, Grandma, absolutely nothing,' he called back.

'Is it time for my medicine yet?'

'No, Grandma, not for about half an hour.'

'Well, just see you don't forget it.'

'I won't, Grandma,' George answered. 'I promise I won't.'

Animal Pills

At this point, George suddenly had an extra good wheeze. Although the medicine cupboard in the house was forbidden ground, what about the medicines his father kept on the shelf in the shed next to the henhouse? The animal medicines?

What about *those*?

Nobody had ever told him he mustn't touch *them*.

Let's face it, George said to himself, hair-spray and shaving-cream and shoe-polish are all very well and they will no doubt cause some splendid explosions inside the old geezer, but what the magic mixture now needs is a touch of the real stuff, real pills and real tonics, to give it punch and muscle.

George picked up the heavy three-quarters full saucepan and carried it out of the back door. He crossed the farmyard and headed straight for the shed alongside the henhouse. He knew his father wouldn't be there. He was out haymaking in one of the meadows.

George entered the dusty old shed and put the saucepan on the bench. Then he looked up at the medicine shelf. There were five big bottles there. Two were full of pills, two were full of runny stuff and one was full of powder.

'I'll use them all,' George said. 'Grandma needs them. Boy, does she need them!'

The first bottle he took down contained an orange-coloured powder. The label said, FOR CHICKENS WITH FOUL PEST, HEN GRIPE,

SORE BEAKS, GAMMY LEGS, COCKERELITIS, EGG TROUBLE, BROODINESS OR LOSS OF FEATHERS. MIX ONE SPOONFUL ONLY WITH EACH BUCKET OF FEED.

'Well,' George said aloud to himself as he tipped in the whole bottleful, 'the old bird won't be losing any feathers after she's had a dose of this.'

The next bottle he took down had about five hundred gigantic purple pills in it. FOR HORSES WITH HOARSE THROATS, it said on the label. THE HOARSE-THROATED HORSE SHOULD SUCK ONE PILL TWICE A DAY.

'Grandma may not have a hoarse throat,' George said, 'but she's certainly got a sharp tongue. Maybe they'll cure that instead.' Into the saucepan went the five hundred gigantic purple pills.

Then there was a bottle of thick yellowish liquid. FOR COWS, BULLS AND BULLOCKS, the label said. WILL CURE COW POX, COW MANGE, CRUMPLED HORNS, BAD BREATH IN BULLS, EARACHE, TOOTHACHE, HEADACHE, HOOF-ACHE, TAILACHE AND SORE UDDERS.

'That grumpy old cow in the living-room has every one of those rotten illnesses,' George said. 'She'll need it all.' With a slop and a gurgle, the yellow liquid splashed into the now nearly full saucepan.

The next bottle contained a brilliant red liquid. SHEEPDIP, it said on the label. FOR SHEEP WITH SHEEPROT AND FOR GETTING RID OF TICKS AND FLEAS. MIX ONE SPOONFUL IN ONE GAL-LON OF WATER AND SLOSH IT OVER THE SHEEP. CAUTION, DO NOT MAKE THE MIX-TURE ANY STRONGER OR THE WOOL WILL FALL OUT AND THE ANIMAL WILL BE NAKED.

'By gum,' said George, 'how I'd love to walk in and slosh it all over old Grandma and watch the ticks and fleas go jumping off her. But I can't. I mustn't. So she'll have to drink it instead.' He poured the bright red medicine into the saucepan.

The last bottle on the shelf was full of pale green pills. PIG PILLS, the label announced. FOR

PIGS WITH PORK PRICKLES, TENDER TROT-
TERS, BRISTLE BLIGHT AND SWINE SICKNESS.
GIVE ONE PILL PER DAY. IN SEVERE CASES
TWO PILLS MAY BE GIVEN, BUT MORE THAN
THAT WILL MAKE THE PIG ROCK AND ROLL.

'Just the stuff,' said George, 'for that miserable
old pig back there in the house. She'll need a very
big dose.' He tipped all the green pills, hundreds
and hundreds of them, into the saucepan.

There was an old stick lying on the bench that
had been used for stirring paint. George picked it

up and started to stir his marvellous concoction. The mixture was as thick as cream, and as he stirred and stirred, many wonderful colours rose up from the depths and blended together, pinks, blues, greens, yellows and browns.

George went on stirring until it was all well mixed, but even so there were still hundreds of pills lying on the bottom that hadn't melted. And there was his mother's splendid powder-puff floating on the surface. 'I shall have to boil it all up,' George said. 'One good quick boil on the stove is all it needs.' And with that he staggered back towards the house with the enormous heavy saucepan.

On the way, he passed the garage, so he went in to see if he could find any other interesting things. He added the following:

Half a pint of ENGINE OIL – to keep Grandma's engine going smoothly.

Some ANTI-FREEZE – to keep her radiator from freezing up in winter.

A handful of GREASE – to grease her creaking joints.

Then back to the kitchen.

The Cook-up

In the kitchen, George put the saucepan on the stove and turned up the gas flame underneath it as high as it would go.

'George!' came the awful voice from the next room. 'It's time for my medicine!'

'Not yet, Grandma,' George called back. 'There's still twenty minutes before eleven o'clock.'

'What mischief are you up to in there now?' Granny screeched. 'I hear noises.'

George thought it best not to answer this one. He found a long wooden spoon in a kitchen drawer and began stirring hard. The stuff in the pot got hotter and hotter.

Soon the marvellous mixture began to froth and foam. A rich blue smoke, the colour of peacocks, rose from the surface of the liquid, and a fiery fearsome smell filled the kitchen. It made George choke and splutter. It was a smell unlike any he had smelled before. It was a brutal and bewitching smell, spicy and staggering, fierce and frenzied, full of wizardry and magic. Whenever he got a whiff of it up his nose, firecrackers went off in his skull and electric prickles ran along the backs of his legs. It was wonderful to stand there stirring this amazing mixture and to watch it smoking blue and bubbling and frothing and foaming as though it were alive. At one point, he could have sworn he saw bright sparks flashing in the swirling foam.

And suddenly, George found himself dancing around the steaming pot, chanting strange words that came into his head out of nowhere:

'Fiery broth and witch's brew
Foamy froth and riches blue
Fume and spume and spoondrift spray
Fizzle swizzle shout hooray
Watch it sloshing, swashing, sploshing
Hear it hissing, squishing, spissing
Grandma better start to pray.'

Brown Paint

George turned off the heat under the saucepan. He must leave plenty of time for it to cool down.

When all the steam and froth had gone away, he peered into the giant pan to see what colour the great medicine now was. It was a deep and brilliant blue.

'It needs more brown in it,' George said. 'It simply must be brown or she'll get suspicious.'

George ran outside and dashed into his father's toolshed where all the paints were kept. There was a row of cans on the shelf, all colours, black, green, red, pink, white and brown. He reached for the can of brown. The label said simply DARK BROWN GLOSS PAINT ONE QUART. He took a screwdriver and prised off the lid. The can was three-quarters full. He rushed it back to the kitchen. He poured the whole lot into the saucepan. The saucepan was now full to the brim. Very gently, George stirred the paint into the mixture with the long wooden spoon. Ah-ha! It was all turning brown! A lovely rich creamy brown!

'Where's that medicine of mine, boy?!' came

the voice from the living-room. 'You're forgetting me! You're doing it on purpose! I shall tell your mother!'

'I'm not forgetting you, Grandma,' George called back. 'I'm thinking of you all the time. But there are still ten minutes to go.'

'You're a nasty little maggot!' the voice screeched back. 'You're a lazy and disobedient little worm, and you're growing too fast.'

George fetched the bottle of Grandma's real medicine from the sideboard. He took out the cork and tipped it all down the sink. He then filled the bottle with his own magic mixture by dipping a small jug into the saucepan and using it as a pourer. He replaced the cork.

Had it cooled down enough yet? Not quite. He held the bottle under the cold tap for a couple of minutes. The label came off in the wet but that didn't matter. He dried the bottle with a dish-cloth.

All was now ready!

This was it!

The great moment had arrived!

'Medicine time, Grandma!' he called out.

'I should hope so, too,' came the grumpy reply.

The silver tablespoon in which the medicine was always given lay ready on the kitchen side-board. George picked it up.

Holding the spoon in one hand and the bottle in the other, he advanced into the living-room.

Grandma Gets the Medicine

Grandma sat hunched in her chair by the window. The wicked little eyes followed George closely as he crossed the room towards her.

'You're late,' she snapped.

'I don't think I am, Grandma.'

'Don't interrupt me in the middle of a sentence!' she shouted.

'But you'd finished your sentence, Grandma.'

'There you go again!' she cried. 'Always interrupting and arguing. You really are a tiresome little boy. What's the time?'

'It's exactly eleven o'clock, Grandma.'

'You're lying as usual. Stop talking so much and give me my medicine. Shake the bottle first. Then pour it into the spoon and make sure it's a whole spoonful.'

'Are you going to gulp it all down in one go?' George asked her. 'Or will you sip it?'

'What I do is none of your business,' the old woman said. 'Fill the spoon.'

As George removed the cork and began very

38

slowly to pour the thick brown stuff into the spoon, he couldn't help thinking back upon all the mad and marvellous things that had gone into the making of this crazy stuff – the shaving soap, the hair remover, the dandruff cure, the automatic washing-machine powder, the flea powder for dogs, the shoe-polish, the black pepper, the horseradish sauce and all the rest of them, not to mention the powerful animal pills and powders and liquids . . . and the brown paint.

'Open your mouth wide, Grandma,' he said, 'and I'll pop it in.'

The old hag opened her small wrinkled mouth, showing disgusting pale brown teeth.

'Here we go!' George cried out. 'Swallow it down!' He pushed the spoon well into her mouth and tipped the mixture down her throat. Then he stepped back to watch the result.

It was worth watching.

Grandma yelled '*Oweeeee!*' and her whole body shot up *whoosh* into the air. It was exactly as though someone had pushed an electric wire through the underneath of her chair and switched on the current. Up she went like a jack-in-the-box . . . and she didn't come down . . . she stayed there . . . suspended in mid-air . . . about two feet up . . . still in a sitting position . . . but

rigid now ... frozen ... quivering ... the eyes
bulging ... the hair standing straight up on end.

'Is something wrong, Grandma?' George asked
her politely. 'Are you all right?'

Suspended up there in space, the old girl was
beyond speaking.

The shock that George's marvellous mixture
had given her must have been tremendous.

You'd have thought she'd swallowed a red-hot
poker the way she took off from that chair.

Then down she came again with a *plop*, back into her seat.

'Call the fire brigade!' she shouted suddenly. 'My stomach's on fire!'

'It's just the medicine, Grandma,' George said. 'It's good strong stuff.'

'Fire!' the old woman yelled. 'Fire in the basement! Get a bucket! Man the hoses! Do something quick!'

'Cool it, Grandma,' George said. But he got a bit of a shock when he saw the smoke coming out of her mouth and out of her nostrils. Clouds of black smoke were coming out of her nose and blowing around the room.

'By golly, you really are on fire,' George said.

'Of course I'm on fire!' she yelled. 'I'll be burned to a crisp! I'll be fried to a frizzle! I'll be boiled like a beetroot!'

George ran into the kitchen and came back with a jug of water. 'Open your mouth, Grandma!' he cried. He could hardly see her for the smoke, but he managed to pour half a jugful down her throat. A sizzling sound, the kind you get if you hold a hot frying-pan under a cold tap, came up from deep down in Grandma's stomach. The old hag bucked and shied and snorted. She gasped and gurgled. Spouts of water came

41

shooting out of her. And the smoke cleared away.

'The fire's out,' George announced proudly. 'You'll be all right now, Grandma.'

'*All right?*' she yelled. 'Who's *all right?* There's jacky-jumpers in my tummy! There's squigglers in my belly! There's bangers in my bottom!' She began bouncing up and down in the chair. Quite obviously she was not very comfortable.

'You'll find it's doing you a lot of good, that medicine, Grandma,' George said.

'*Good?*' she screamed. 'Doing me *good?* It's *killing* me!'

Then she began to bulge.

She was swelling!

She was puffing up all over!

Someone was pumping her up, that's how it looked!

Was she going to explode?

Her face was turning from purple to green!

But wait! She had a puncture somewhere! George could hear the hiss of escaping air. She stopped swelling. She was going down. She was slowly getting thinner again, shrinking back and back slowly to her shrivelly old self.

'How's things, Grandma?' George said.

No answer.

Then a funny thing happened. Grandma's

body gave a sudden sharp twist and a sudden sharp jerk and she flipped herself clear out of the chair and landed neatly on her two feet on the carpet.

'That's terrific, Grandma!' George cried. 'You haven't stood up like that for years! Look at you! You're standing up all on your own and you're not even using a stick!'

Grandma didn't even hear him. The frozen pop-eyed look was back with her again now. She was miles away in another world.

Marvellous medicine, George told himself. He found it fascinating to stand there watching what it was doing to the old hag. What next? he wondered.

He soon found out.

Suddenly she began to grow.

It was quite slow at first . . . just a very gradual inching upwards . . . up, up, up . . . inch by inch . . . getting taller and taller . . . about an inch every few seconds . . . and in the beginning George didn't notice it.

But when she had passed the five foot six mark and was going on up towards being six feet tall, George gave a jump and shouted, 'Hey, Grandma! You're *growing*! You're *going up*! Hang on, Grandma! You'd better stop now or you'll be hitting the ceiling!'

But Grandma didn't stop.

It was a truly fantastic sight, this ancient scrawny old woman getting taller and taller, longer and longer, thinner and thinner, as though she were a piece of elastic being pulled upwards by invisible hands.

When the top of her head actually touched the ceiling, George thought she was bound to stop.

But she didn't.

There was a sort of scrunching noise, and bits of plaster and cement came raining down.

'Hadn't you better stop now, Grandma?' George said. 'Daddy's just had this whole room repainted.'

But there was no stopping her now.

Soon, her head and shoulders had completely disappeared through the ceiling and she was still going.

George dashed upstairs to his own bedroom and there she was coming up through the floor like a mushroom.

'Whoopee!' she shouted, finding her voice at last. 'Hallelujah, here I come!'

'Steady on, Grandma,' George said.

'With a heigh-nonny-no and up we go!' she shouted. 'Just watch me grow!'

'This is *my* room,' George said. 'Look at the mess you're making.'

'Terrific medicine!' she cried. 'Give me some more!'

She's dotty as a doughnut, George thought.

'Come on, boy! Give me some more!' she yelled. 'Dish it out! I'm slowing down!'

George was still clutching the medicine bottle in one hand and the spoon in the other. Oh well, he thought, why not? He poured out a second dose and popped it into her mouth.

'*Oweee!*' she screamed and up she went again. Her feet were still on the floor downstairs in the living-room but her head was moving quickly towards the ceiling of the bedroom.

'I'm on my way now, boy!' she called down to George. 'Just watch me go!'

'That's the attic above you, Grandma!' George called out. 'I'd keep out of there! It's full of bugs and bogles!'

Crash! The old girl's head went through the ceiling as though it were butter.

George stood in his bedroom gazing at the shambles. There was a big hole in the floor and another in the ceiling, and sticking up like a post between the two was the middle part of Grandma. Her legs were in the room below, her head in the attic.

'I'm still going!' came the old screechy voice from up above. 'Give me another dose, my boy, and let's go through the roof!'

'No, Grandma, no!' George called back. 'You're busting up the whole house!'

'To heck with the house!' she shouted. 'I want some fresh air! I haven't been outside for twenty years!'

'By golly, she *is* going through the roof!' George told himself. He ran downstairs. He rushed out of the back door into the yard. It would be simply awful, he thought, if she bashed up the roof as well. His father would be furious. And he, George, would get the blame. *He* had made the medicine. *He* had given her too much. 'Don't come through the roof, Grandma,' he prayed. 'Please don't.'

The Brown Hen

George stood in the farmyard looking up at the roof. The old farmhouse had a fine roof of pale red tiles and tall chimneys.

There was no sign of Grandma. There was only a song-thrush sitting on one of the chimney-pots, singing a song. The old wurzel's got stuck in the attic, George thought. Thank goodness for that.

Suddenly a tile came clattering down from the roof and fell into the yard. The song-thrush took off fast and flew away.

Then another tile came down.

Then half a dozen more.

And then, very slowly, like some weird monster rising up from the deep, Grandma's head came through the roof . . .

Then her scrawny neck . . .

And the tops of her shoulders . . .

'How'm I doing, boy!' she shouted. 'How's that for a bash up?'

'Don't you think you'd better stop now, Grandma?' George called out . . .

'I have stopped!' she answered. 'I feel terrific!

Didn't I tell you I had magic powers! Didn't I warn you I had wizardry in the tips of my fingers! But you wouldn't listen to me, would you? You wouldn't listen to your old Grandma!'

'*You* didn't do it, Grandma,' George shouted back to her. '*I* did it! I made you a new medicine!'

'*A new medicine? You?* What rubbish!' she yelled.

'I did! I did!' George shouted.

'You're lying as usual!' Grandma yelled. 'You're always lying!'

'I'm not lying, Grandma. I swear I'm not.'

The wrinkled old face high up on the roof stared down suspiciously at George. 'Are you telling me you actually made a new medicine all by yourself?' she shouted.

'Yes, Grandma, all by myself.'

'I don't believe you,' she answered. 'But I'm very comfortable up here. Fetch me a cup of tea.'

A brown hen was pecking about in the yard close to where George was standing. The hen gave him an idea. Quickly, he uncorked the medicine bottle and poured some of the brown stuff into the spoon. 'Watch this, Grandma!' he shouted. He crouched down, holding out the spoon to the hen.

'Chicken,' he said. 'Chick-chick-chicken. Come here. Have some of this.'

Chickens are stupid birds, and very greedy. They think everything is food. This one thought the spoon was full of corn. It hopped over. It put its head on one side and looked at the spoon. 'Come on, chicken,' George said. 'Good chicken. Chick-chick-chick.'

The brown hen stretched out its neck towards the spoon and went *peck*. It got a beakful of medicine.

The effect was electric.

'*Oweee!*' shrieked the hen and it shot straight up into the air like a rocket. It went as high as the house.

Then down it came again into the yard, *splosh*. And there it sat with its feathers all sticking straight out from its body. There was a look of amazement on its silly face. George stood watching it. Grandma up on the roof was watching it, too.

The hen got to its feet. It was rather shaky. It was making funny gurgling noises in its throat. Its beak was opening and shutting. It seemed like a pretty sick hen.

'You've done it in, you stupid boy!' Grandma shouted. 'That hen's going to die! Your father'll be after you now! He'll give you socks and serve you right!'

All of a sudden, black smoke started pouring out of the hen's beak.

'It's on fire!' Grandma yelled. 'The hen's on fire!'

George ran to the water-trough to get a bucket of water.

'That hen'll be roasted and ready for eating any moment!' Grandma shouted.

George sloshed the bucket of water over the hen. There was a sizzling sound and the smoke went away.

'Old hen's laid its last egg!' Grandma shouted. 'Hens don't do any laying after they've been on fire!'

Now that the fire was out, the hen seemed better. It stood up properly. It flapped its wings. Then it crouched down low to the ground, as though getting ready to jump. It did jump. It jumped high in the air and turned a complete somersault, then landed back on its feet.

'It's a circus hen!' Grandma shouted from the rooftop. 'It's a flipping acrobat!'

Now the hen began to grow.

George had been waiting for this to happen. 'It's growing!' he yelled. 'It's growing, Grandma! Look, it's growing!'

Bigger and bigger . . . taller and taller it grew. Soon the hen was four or five times its normal size.

'Can you see it, Grandma?!' George shouted.

'I can see it, boy!' the old girl shouted back. 'I'm watching it!'

George was hopping about from one foot to the other with excitement, pointing at the enormous hen and shouting, 'It's had the magic medicine, Grandma, and it's growing just like you did!'

But there was a difference between the way the hen was growing and the way Grandma grew. When Grandma grew taller and taller, she got

thinner and thinner. The hen didn't. It stayed nice and plump all along.

Soon it was taller than George, but it didn't stop there. It went right on growing until it was about as big as a horse. Then it stopped.

'Doesn't it look marvellous, Grandma!' George shouted.

'It's not as tall as me!' Grandma sang out. 'Compared with me, that hen is titchy small! I am the tallest of them all!'

The Pig, the Bullocks, the Sheep, the Pony and the Nanny-goat

At that moment, George's mother came back from shopping in the village. She drove her car into the yard and got out. She was carrying a bottle of milk in one hand and a bag of groceries in the other.

The first thing she saw was the gigantic brown hen towering over little George. She dropped the bottle of milk.

Then Grandma started shouting at her from the rooftop, and when she looked up and saw Grandma's head sticking up through the tiles, she dropped the bag of groceries.

'How about that then, eh, Mary?' Grandma shouted. 'I'll bet you've never seen a hen as big as that! That's George's giant hen, that is!'

'But . . . but . . . but . . .' stammered George's mother.

'It's George's magic medicine!' Grandma shouted. 'We've both of us had it, the hen and I!'

'But how in the world did you get up on the roof?' cried the mother.

'I didn't!' cackled the old woman. 'My feet are still standing on the floor in the living-room!'

This was too much for George's mother to understand. She just goggled and gaped. She looked as though she was going to faint.

A second later, George's father appeared. His name was Mr Killy Kranky. Mr Kranky was a small man with bandy legs and a huge head. He was a kind father to George, but he was not an easy person to live with because even the smallest things got him all worked up and excited. The hen standing in the yard was certainly not a small thing, and when Mr Kranky saw it he started jumping about as though something was burning his feet. 'Great heavens!' he cried, waving his arms. 'What's this? What's happened? Where did it come from? It's a giant hen! Who did it?'

'I did,' George said.

'Look at *me*!' Grandma shouted from the rooftop. 'Never mind about the hen! What about *me*?'

Mr Kranky looked up and saw Grandma. 'Shut up, Grandma,' he said. It didn't seem to surprise him that the old girl was sticking up through the roof. It was the hen that excited him. He had never seen anything like it. But then who had?

'It's fantastic!' Mr Kranky shouted, dancing round and round. 'It's colossal! It's gigantic! It's tremendous! It's a miracle! How did you do it, George?'

George started telling his father about the magic medicine. While he was doing this, the big brown hen sat down in the middle of the yard and went *cluck-cluck-cluck* . . . *cluck-cluck-cluck-cluck-cluck*.

Everyone stared at it.

When it stood up again, there was a brown egg lying there. The egg was the size of a football.

'That egg would make scrambled eggs for twenty people!' Mrs Kranky said.

'George!' Mr Kranky shouted. 'How much of this medicine have you got?'

'Lots,' George said. 'There's a big saucepanful in the kitchen, and this bottle here's nearly full.'

'Come with me!' Mr Kranky yelled, grabbing George by the arm. 'Bring the medicine! For years and years I've been trying to breed bigger and bigger animals. Bigger bulls for beef. Bigger pigs for pork. Bigger sheep for mutton . . .'

They went to the pigsty first.

George gave a spoonful of medicine to the pig.

The pig blew smoke from its nose and jumped about all over the place. Then it grew and grew.

In the end, it looked like this . . .

They went to the herd of fine black bullocks that Mr Kranky was trying to fatten for the market.

George gave each of them some medicine, and this is what happened . . .

Then the sheep . . .

He gave some to his grey pony, Jack Frost . . .

And finally, just for fun, he gave some to Alma, the nanny-goat . . .

A Crane for Grandma

Grandma, from high up on the rooftop, could see everything that was going on and she didn't like what she saw. She wanted to be the centre of attention and nobody was taking the slightest notice of her. George and Mr Kranky were running round and getting excited about the enormous animals. Mrs Kranky was washing up in the kitchen, and Grandma was all alone on the rooftop.

'Hey you!' she yelled. 'George! Get me a cup of tea this minute, you idle little beast!'

'Don't listen to the old goat,' Mr Kranky said. 'She's stuck where she is and a good thing, too.'

'But we can't leave her up there, Dad,' George said. 'What if it rains?'

'George!' Grandma yelled. 'Oh, you horrible little boy! You disgusting little worm! Fetch me a cup of tea at once and a slice of currant cake!'

'We'll have to get her out, Dad,' George said. 'She won't give us any peace if we don't.'

Mrs Kranky came outside and she agreed with George. 'She's my own mother,' she said.

'She's a pain in the neck,' Mr Kranky said.

'I don't care,' Mrs Kranky said. 'I'm not leaving my own mother sticking up through the roof for the rest of her life.'

So in the end, Mr Kranky telephoned the Crane Company and asked them to send their biggest crane out to the house at once.

The crane arrived one hour later. It was on

wheels and there were two men inside it. The crane men climbed up on to the roof and put ropes under Grandma's arms. Then she was lifted right up through the roof . . .

In a way, the medicine had done Grandma good. It had not made her any less grumpy or bad-tempered, but it seemed to have cured all her aches and pains, and she was suddenly as frisky as a ferret. As soon as the crane had lowered her to the ground, she ran over to George's huge pony, Jack Frost, and jumped on to his back. This ancient old hag, who was now as tall as a house, then galloped about the farm on the gigantic pony, jumping over trees and sheds and shouting, 'Out of my way! Clear the decks! Stand back, all

you miserable midgets or I'll trample you to
death!' and other silly things like that.

But because Grandma was now much too tall
to get back into the house, she had to sleep that
night in the hay-barn with the mice and the rats.

Mr Kranky's Great Idea

The next day, George's father came down to breakfast in a state of greater excitement than ever. 'I've been awake all night thinking about it!' he cried.

'About what, Dad?' George asked him.

'About your marvellous medicine, of course! We can't stop now, my boy! We must start making more of it at once! More and more and more!'

The giant saucepan had been completely emptied the day before because there had been so many sheep and pigs and cows and bullocks to be dosed.

'But why do we need more, Dad?' George asked. 'We've done all our own animals and we've made Grandma feel as frisky as a ferret even though she does have to sleep in the barn.'

'My dear boy,' cried Mr Killy Kranky, 'we need barrels and barrels of it! Tons and tons! Then we will sell it to every farmer in the world so that all of them can have giant animals! We will build a Marvellous Medicine Factory and sell the stuff in bottles at five pounds a time. We will become rich and you will become famous!'

'But wait a minute, Dad,' George said.

'There's no waiting!' cried Mr Kranky, working himself up so much that he put butter in his coffee and milk on his toast. 'Don't you understand what this tremendous invention of yours is going to do to the world! Nobody will ever go hungry again!'

'Why won't they?' asked George.

'Because one giant cow will give fifty buckets of milk a day!' cried Mr Kranky, waving his arms. 'One giant chicken will make a hundred fried chicken dinners, and one giant pig will give you a thousand pork chops! It's tremendous, my dear boy! It's fantastic! It'll change the world.'

'But wait a minute, Dad,' George said again.

'Don't keep saying wait a minute!' shouted Mr

Kranky. 'There isn't a minute to *wait*! We must get cracking at once!'

'Do calm down, my dear,' Mrs Kranky said from the other end of the table. 'And stop putting marmalade on your cornflakes.'

'The heck with my cornflakes!' cried Mr Kranky, leaping up from his chair. 'Come on, George! Let's get going! And the first thing we'll do is to make one more saucepanful as a tester.'

'But Dad,' said little George. 'The trouble is . . .'

'There won't be any trouble, my boy!' cried Mr Kranky. 'How can there possibly be any trouble? All you've got to do is put the same stuff into the saucepan as you did yesterday. And while you're doing it, I'll write down each and every item. That's how we'll get the magic recipe!'

'But Dad,' George said. 'Please listen to me.'

'Why don't you listen to him?' Mrs Kranky said. 'The boy's trying to tell you something.'

But Mr Kranky was too excited to listen to anyone except himself. 'And then,' he cried, 'when the new mixture is ready, we'll test it out on an old hen just to make absolutely sure we've got it right, and after that we'll all shout hooray and build the giant factory!'

'But Dad . . .'

'Come on then, what is it you want to say?'

'I can't possibly remember all the hundreds of things I put into the saucepan to make the medicine,' George said.

'Of course you can, my dear boy,' cried Mr Kranky. 'I'll help you! I'll jog your memory! You'll get it in the end, you see if you don't! Now then, what was the very first thing you put in?'

'I went up to the bathroom first,' George said. 'I used a lot of things in the bathroom and on Mummy's dressing-table.'

'Come on, then!' cried Mr Killy Kranky. 'Up we go to the bathroom!'

When they got there, they found, of course, a whole lot of empty tubes and empty aerosols and empty bottles. 'That's great,' said Mr Kranky. 'That tells us exactly what you used. If anything is empty, it means you used it.'

So Mr Kranky started making a list of everything that was empty in the bathroom. Then they went to Mrs Kranky's dressing-table. 'A box of powder,' said Mr Kranky, writing it down. 'Helga's hairset. Flowers of Turnips perfume. Terrific. This is going to be easy. Where did you go next?'

'To the laundry-room,' George said. 'But are you sure you haven't missed anything out up here, Dad?'

'That's up to you, my boy,' Mr Kranky said. 'Have I?'

'I don't think so,' George said. So down they went to the laundry-room and once again Mr Kranky wrote down the names of all the empty bottles and cans. 'My goodness me, what a mass of stuff you used!' he cried. 'No wonder it did magic things! Is that the lot?'

'No, Dad, it's not,' George said, and he led his father out to the shed where the animal medicines were kept and showed him the five big empty bottles up on the shelf. Mr Kranky wrote down all their names.

'Anything else?' Mr Kranky asked.

Little George scratched his head and thought and thought but he couldn't remember having put anything else in.

Mr Killy Kranky leapt into his car and drove down to the village and bought new bottles and tubes and cans of everything on his list. He then went to the vet and got a fresh supply of all the animal medicines George had used.

'Now show me how you did it, George,' he said. 'Come along. Show me exactly how you mixed them all together.'

Marvellous Medicine
Number Two

They were in the kitchen now and the big saucepan was on the stove. All the things Mr Kranky had bought were lined up near the sink.

'Come along, my boy!' cried Mr Killy Kranky. 'Which one did you put in first?'

'This one,' George said. 'Golden Gloss Hair Shampoo.' He emptied the bottle into the pan.

'Now the toothpaste,' George went on . . . 'And the shaving soap . . . and the face cream . . . and the nail varnish . . .'

'Keep at it, my boy!' cried Mr Kranky, dancing round the kitchen. 'Keep putting them in! Don't stop! Don't pause! Don't hesitate! It's a pleasure, my dear fellow, to watch you work!'

One by one, George poured and squeezed the things into the saucepan. With everything so close at hand, the whole job didn't take him more than ten minutes. But when it was all done, the saucepan didn't somehow seem to be quite as full as it had been the first time.

'*Now* what did you do?' cried Mr Kranky.

'Did you stir it?'

'I boiled it,' George said. 'But not for long. And I stirred it as well.'

So Mr Kranky lit the gas under the saucepan and George stirred the mixture with the same long wooden spoon he had used before. 'It's not brown enough,' George said. 'Wait a minute! I know what I've forgotten!'

'What?' cried Mr Kranky. 'Tell me, quick! Because if we've forgotten even one tiny thing, then it won't work! At least not in the same way.'

'A quart of brown gloss paint,' George said. 'That's what I've forgotten.'

Mr Killy Kranky shot out of the house and into his car like a rocket. He sped down to the village and bought the paint and rushed back again. He opened the can in the kitchen and handed it to George. George poured the paint into the saucepan.

'Ah-ha, that's better,' George said. 'That's more like the right colour.'

'It's boiling!' cried Mr Kranky. 'It's boiling and bubbling, George! Is it ready yet?'

'It's ready,' George said. 'At least I hope it is.'

'Right!' shouted Mr Kranky, hopping about. 'Let's test it! Let's give some to a chicken!'

'My heavens alive, why don't you calm down a

bit?' Mrs Kranky said, coming into the kitchen.

'*Calm down?*' cried Mr Kranky. 'You expect me to *calm down* and here we are mixing up the greatest medicine ever discovered in the history of the world! Come along, George! Dip a cupful out of the saucepan and get a spoon and we'll give some to a chicken just to make absolutely certain we've got the correct mixture.'

Outside in the yard, there were several chickens that hadn't had any of George's Marvellous Medicine Number One. They were pecking about in the dirt in that silly way chickens do.

George crouched down, holding out a spoonful of Marvellous Medicine Number Two. 'Come on, chicken,' he said. 'Good chicken. Chick-chick-chick.'

A white chicken with black specks on its feathers looked up at George. It walked over to the spoon and went *peck*.

The effect that Medicine Number Two had on this chicken was not quite the same as the effect produced by Medicine Number One, but it was very interesting. '*Whooosh!*' shrieked the chicken and it shot six feet up in the air and came down again. Then *sparks* came flying out of its beak, bright yellow sparks of fire, as though someone was sharpening a knife on a grindstone inside its tummy. Then its legs began to grow longer. Its body stayed the same size but the two thin yellow legs got longer and longer and longer . . . and longer still . . .

'What's happening to it?' cried Mr Killy Kranky.

'Something's wrong,' George said.

The legs went on growing and the more they grew, the higher up into the air went the chicken's body. When the legs were about fifteen feet long, they stopped growing. The chicken looked perfectly absurd with its long long legs and its ordinary little body perched high up on top. It was like a chicken on stilts.

'Oh my sainted aunts!' cried Mr Killy Kranky. 'We've got it wrong! This chicken's no good to anybody! It's all legs! No one wants chickens' legs!'

'I must have left something out,' George said.

'I *know* you left something out!' cried Mr Kranky. 'Think, boy, think! What was it you left out?'

'I've got it!' said George.

'What was it, quick?'

'Flea powder for dogs,' George said.

'You mean you put *flea* powder in the first one?'

'Yes, Dad, I did. A whole carton of it.'

'Then that's the answer!'

'Wait a minute,' said George. 'Did we have brown shoe-polish on our list?'

'We did not,' said Mr Kranky.

'I used that, too,' said George.

'Well, no *wonder* it went wrong,' said Mr Kranky. He was already running to his car, and soon he was heading down to the village to buy more flea powder and more shoe-polish.

Marvellous Medicine
Number Three

'Here it is!' cried Mr Killy Kranky, rushing into the kitchen. 'One carton of flea powder for dogs and one tin of brown shoe-polish!'

George poured the flea powder into the giant saucepan. Then he scooped the shoe-polish out of its tin and added that as well.

'Stir it up, George!' shouted Mr Kranky. 'Give it another boil! We've got it this time! I'll bet we've got it!'

After Marvellous Medicine Number Three had been boiled and stirred, George took a cupful of it out into the yard to try it on another chicken. Mr Kranky ran after him, flapping his arms and hopping with excitement. 'Come and watch this one!' he called out to Mrs Kranky. 'Come and watch us turning an ordinary chicken into a lovely great big one that lays eggs as large as footballs!'

'I hope you do better than last time,' said Mrs Kranky, following them out.

'Come on, chicken,' said George, holding out a spoonful of Medicine Number Three. 'Good chicken. Chick-chick-chick-chick-chick. Have some of this lovely medicine.'

A magnificent black cockerel with a scarlet comb came stepping over. The cockerel looked at the spoon and it went *peck*.

'*Cock-a-doodle-do!*' squawked the cockerel, shooting up into the air and coming down again.

'Watch him now!' cried Mr Kranky. 'Watch him grow! Any moment he's going to start getting bigger and bigger!'

Mr Killy Kranky, Mrs Kranky and little George stood in the yard staring at the black cockerel. The cockerel stood quite still. It looked as though it had a headache.

'What's happening to its neck?' Mrs Kranky said.

'It's getting longer,' George said.

'I'll say it's getting longer,' Mrs Kranky said.

Mr Kranky, for once, said nothing.

'Last time it was the legs,' Mrs Kranky said.

'Now it's the neck. Who wants a chicken with a long neck? You can't eat a chicken's neck.'

It was an extraordinary sight. The cockerel's body hadn't grown at all. But the neck was now about six feet long.

'All right, George,' Mr Kranky said. 'What else have you forgotten?'

'I don't know,' George said.

'Oh yes you do,' Mr Kranky said. 'Come along, boy, *think*. There's probably just one vital thing missing and you've got to remember it.'

'I put in some engine oil from the garage,' George said. 'Did you have that on your list?'

'Eureka!' cried Mr Kranky. 'That's the answer! How much did you put in?'

'Half a pint,' George said.

Mr Kranky ran to the garage and found another half-pint of oil. 'And some anti-freeze,' George called after him. 'I sloshed in a bit of anti-freeze.'

Marvellous Medicine
Number Four

Back in the kitchen once again, George, with Mr Kranky watching him anxiously, tipped half a pint of engine oil and some anti-freeze into the giant saucepan.

'Boil it up again!' cried Mr Kranky. 'Boil it and stir it!'

George boiled it and stirred it.

'You'll never get it right,' said Mrs Kranky. 'Don't forget you don't just have to have the same things but you've got to have exactly the same *amounts* of those things. And how can you possibly do that?'

'You keep out of this!' cried Mr Kranky. 'We're doing fine! We've got it this time, you see if we haven't!'

This was George's Marvellous Medicine Number Four, and when it had boiled for a couple of minutes, George once again carried a cupful of it out into the yard. Mr Kranky ran after him. Mrs Kranky followed more slowly. 'You're going to have some mighty queer chickens around here if you go on like this,' she said.

'Dish it out, George!' cried Mr Kranky. 'Give a spoonful to that one over there!' He pointed to a brown hen.

George knelt down and held out the spoon with the new medicine in it. 'Chick-chick,' he said. 'Try some of this.'

The brown hen walked over and looked at the spoon. Then it went *peck*.

'*Owch!*' it said. Then a funny whistling noise came out of its beak.

'Watch it grow!' shouted Mr Kranky.

'Don't be too sure,' said Mrs Kranky. 'Why is it whistling like that?'

'Keep quiet, woman!' cried Mr Kranky. 'Give it a chance!'

They stood there staring at the brown hen.

'It's getting smaller,' George said. 'Look at it, Dad. It's shrinking.'

And indeed it was. In less than a minute, the hen had shrunk so much it was no bigger than a new-hatched chick. It looked ridiculous.

Goodbye Grandma

'There's still something you've left out,' Mr Kranky said.

'I can't think what it could be,' George said.

'Give it up,' Mrs Kranky said. 'Pack it in. You'll never get it right.'

Mr Kranky looked very forlorn.

George looked pretty fed up, too. He was still kneeling on the ground with the spoon in one hand and the cup full of medicine in the other. The ridiculous tiny brown hen was walking slowly away.

At that point, Grandma came striding into the yard. From her enormous height, she glared down at the three people below her and she shouted, 'What's going on around here? Why hasn't anyone brought me my morning cup of tea? It's bad enough having to sleep in the yard with the rats and mice but I'll be blowed if I'm going to starve as well! No tea! No eggs and bacon! No buttered toast!'

'I'm sorry, Mother,' Mrs Kranky said. 'We've been terribly busy. I'll get you something right away.'

'Let George get it, the lazy little brute!'
Grandma shouted.

Just then, the old woman spotted the cup in
George's hand. She bent down and peered into it.
She saw that it was full of brown liquid. It looked

very much like tea. 'Ho-ho!' she cried. 'Ha-ha! So that's your little game, is it! You look after yourself all right, don't you! You make quite sure *you've* got a nice cup of morning tea! But you didn't think to bring one to your poor old Grandma! I always knew you were a selfish pig!'

'No, Grandma,' George said. 'This isn't . . .'

'Don't lie to me, boy!' the enormous old hag shouted. 'Pass it up here this minute!'

'No!' cried Mrs Kranky. 'No, Mother, don't! That's not for you!'

'Now *you're* against me, too!' shouted Grandma. 'My own daughter trying to stop me having my breakfast! Trying to starve me out!'

Mr Kranky looked up at the horrid old woman and he smiled sweetly. 'Of course it's for you, Grandma,' he said. 'You take it and drink it while it's nice and hot.'

'Don't think I won't,' Grandma said, bending down from her great height and reaching out a huge horny hand for the cup. 'Hand it over, George.'

'No, no, Grandma!' George cried out, pulling the cup away. 'You mustn't! You're not to have it!'

'Give it to me, boy!' yelled Grandma.

'Don't!' cried Mrs Kranky. 'That's George's Marvellous . . .'

'Everything's George's round here!' shouted
Grandma. 'George's this, George's that! I'm fed

up with it!' She snatched the cup out of little George's hand and carried it high up out of reach.

'Drink it up, Grandma,' Mr Kranky said, grinning hugely. 'Lovely tea.'

'No!' the other two cried. 'No, no, no!'

But it was too late. The ancient beanpole had already put the cup to her lips, and in one gulp she swallowed everything that was in it.

'Mother!' wailed Mrs Kranky. 'You've just drunk fifty doses of George's Marvellous Medicine Number Four and look what one tiny spoonful did to that little old brown hen!'

But Grandma didn't even hear her. Great clouds of steam were already pouring out of her mouth and she was beginning to whistle.

'This is going to be interesting,' Mr Kranky said, still grinning.

'Now you've done it!' cried Mrs Kranky, glaring at her husband. 'You've cooked the old girl's goose!'

'I didn't do anything,' Mr Kranky said.

'Oh, yes you did! You told her to drink it!'

A tremendous hissing sound was coming from above their heads. Steam was shooting out of Grandma's mouth and nose and ears and whistling as it came.

'She'll feel better after she's let off a bit of steam,' Mr Kranky said.

'She's going to blow up!' Mrs Kranky wailed. 'Her boiler's going to burst!'

'Stand clear,' Mr Kranky said.

George was quite alarmed. He stood up and ran back a few paces. The jets of white steam kept squirting out of the skinny old hag's head, and the whistling was so high and shrill it hurt the ears.

'Call the fire brigade!' cried Mrs Kranky. 'Call the police! Man the hose-pipes!'

'Too late,' said Mr Kranky, looking pleased.

'Grandma!' shrieked Mrs Kranky. 'Mother! Run to the drinking-trough and put your head under the water!'

But even as she spoke, the whistling suddenly stopped and the steam disappeared. That was when Grandma began to get smaller. She had started off with her head as high as the roof of the house, but now she was coming down fast.

'Watch this, George!' Mr Kranky shouted, hopping around the yard and flapping his arms.

'Watch what happens when someone's had fifty spoonfuls instead of one!'

Very soon, Grandma was back to normal height.

'Stop!' cried Mrs Kranky. 'That's just right.'

But she didn't stop. Smaller and smaller she got . . . down and down she went. In another half minute she was no bigger than a bottle of lemonade.

'How d'you feel, Mother?' asked Mrs Kranky anxiously.

Grandma's tiny face still bore the same foul and furious expression it had always had. Her eyes, no bigger now than little keyholes, were blazing with anger. 'How do I *feel*?' she yelled. 'How d'you *think* I feel? How would *you* feel if you'd been a glorious giant a minute ago and suddenly you're a miserable midget?'

'She's still going!' shouted Mr Kranky gleefully. 'She's still getting smaller!'

And by golly, she was.

When she was no bigger than a cigarette, Mrs Kranky made a grab for her. She held her in her hands and she cried, 'How do I stop her getting smaller still?'

'You can't,' said Mr Kranky. 'She's had fifty times the right amount.'

'I *must* stop her!' Mrs Kranky wailed. 'I can hardly see her as it is!'

'Catch hold of each end and pull,' Mr Kranky said.

By then, Grandma was the size of a matchstick and still shrinking fast.

A moment later, she was no bigger than a pin . . .

Then a pumpkin seed . . .

Then . . .

Then . . .

'Where is she?' cried Mrs Kranky. 'I've lost her!'

'Hooray,' said Mr Kranky.

'She's gone! She's disappeared completely!' cried Mrs Kranky.

'That's what happens to you if you're grumpy and bad-tempered,' said Mr Kranky. 'Great medicine of yours, George.'

George didn't know what to think.

For a few minutes, Mrs Kranky kept wandering round with a puzzled look on her face, saying, 'Mother, where are you? Where've you gone?

Where've you got to? How can I find you?' But she calmed down quite quickly. And by lunchtime, she was saying, 'Ah well, I suppose it's all for the best, really. She was a bit of a nuisance around the house, wasn't she?'

'Yes,' Mr Kranky said. 'She most certainly was.'

George didn't say a word. He felt quite trembly. He knew something tremendous had taken place that morning. For a few brief moments he had touched with the very tips of his fingers the edge of a magic world.

SURPRISE

Bet you thought this book had finished.
Well, here's some truly marvellous news – it hasn't!
Turn the page for a whole load of Roald Dahl treats.

YIPPPpEEEe!

Roald Dahl mixed marvellous bedtime drinks for his children and called them witches' potions. They contained ingredients such as tinned peaches blended with milk and pink, blue or green food colouring. Maybe this is where Roald got the idea for George's mischievous potion?

MORE ABOUT
GEORGE'S *Marvellous Medicine*

Roald Dahl loved to put his curious mind to the test by inventing new devices designed to solve the trickiest of problems. When his son, Theo, suffered a serious head injury after a car accident, Roald helped to develop a valve to drain liquid from the brain. Although Theo recovered without needing the valve, it was used to treat 2,000 children.

Weird and wonderful facts about

ROALD DAHL

He was very tall — six feet five and three-quarter inches, or nearly two metres. His nickname in the RAF was Lofty, while Walt Disney called him Stalky (because he was like a beanstalk!).

His nickname at home was the Apple, because he was the apple of his mother's eye (which means her favourite!).

He pretended to have appendicitis when he was nine because he was so homesick in his first two weeks at boarding school. He fooled the matron and the school doctor and was sent home. But he couldn't fool his own doctor, who made him promise never to do it again.

He was a terrible speller, but he liked playing Scrabble.

He didn't like cats — but he did like dogs, birds and goats.

Roald Dahl wrote the screenplay for the James Bond film *You Only Live Twice*.

He once had a tame magpie.

He was a keen photographer at school and, when he was eighteen, won two prizes: one from the Royal Photographic Society in London and another from the Photographic Society of Holland.

GOBBLEFUNK

Roald Dahl loved playing around with words and inventing new ones. In *The BFG* he gave this strange language an even stranger name – Gobblefunk!

BAGGLEPIPES

Bagpipes: famous Scottish wind instrument.

BOGGLEBOX

A school for young children (generally boys).

CRABCRUNCHER

Crabcrunchers live high up on cliffs by the sea. They're very rare.

FROTHBUNGLING

Means stupid.

GLORIUMPTIOUS

Gloriously wonderful.

HUMAN BEAN

This is the name the giants in *The BFG* give to human beings.

JUMPSQUIFFLING

Something absolutely huge.

LIXIVATE

Very gruesome! You are squashed and turned to liquid at the same time.

MUGGLED

To be muggled means to be a bit confused.

QUOGWINKLE

A quogwinkle is an alien from outer space.

SNITCHING

Stealing and thieving.

SNOZZCUMBER

The BFG is forced to eat this disgusting vegetable as it is the only thing that grows in Giant Country. It's knobbly, with black and white stripes, and tastes horrible!

TROGGLEHUMPER

The worst kind of dream: a nightmare.

QUENTINBLAKE

'The finest illustrator of children's books in the world today!' – Roald Dahl

Roald Dahl and Quentin Blake make a perfect partnership of words and illustrations, but when Roald started writing he had many different illustrators. Quentin started working with him in 1976 (the first book he illustrated was *The Enormous Crocodile*, published in 1978) and from then on they worked together until Roald's death. Quentin ended up illustrating all of Roald Dahl's books, with the exception of *The Minpins*.

To begin with, Quentin was a bit nervous about working with such a very famous author, but by the time they collaborated on *The BFG* they had become firm friends. Quentin never knew anything about a new story until the manuscript arrived. 'You'll have some fun with this,' Roald would say – or, 'You'll have some trouble with this.' Quentin would make lots of rough drawings to take along to Gipsy House, where he would show them to Roald and see what he thought. Roald Dahl liked his books to be packed with illustrations – Quentin ended up drawing twice as many pictures for *The BFG* as he had originally been asked for.

Quentin Blake's favourite Roald Dahl book is *The BFG*. When he wasn't quite sure what the BFG's footwear would look like, Roald actually sent one of his old sandals through the post to Quentin – and that's what he drew!

Quentin Blake was born on 16 December 1932. His first drawing was published when he was sixteen, and he has written and illustrated many of his own books, as well as Roald Dahl's. Besides being an illustrator he taught for over twenty years at the Royal College of Art and in 1999 he became the first ever Children's Laureate! Six years later he was awarded a CBE for services to children's literature and in 2013 he was knighted in the New Year's Honours – which means his full title is Sir Quentin Blake, although we can all still go on calling him Quentin as usual.

Find out more at quentinblake.com

Roald Dahl wrote his books in a brick hut, which was built especially for him, on the edge of the orchard at Gipsy House. It was painted white with a yellow front door.

His writing hut was full of gadgets: a chair with a hole cut out of the back (to prevent pressure on his damaged spine), a writing board of exactly the right thickness, tilted at exactly the right angle, and an old suitcase filled with logs for a footrest. His legs were tucked up in a green sleeping bag. He also rigged up a rickety old electric fire on two parallel wires on the ceiling and would pull it towards him if his fingers got cold. Roald wouldn't allow anyone else inside the hut, so it was never cleaned or dusted!

The only thing in the hut that was cleaned regularly was the writing board, which Roald Dahl had designed and made himself. It was covered in green felt and Roald used an old clothes brush to sweep off the bits of rubber from all his rubbings-out. He simply swept them on to the floor and that was where they stayed!

The contents of the writing hut were moved to the Roald Dahl Museum and Story Centre on Great Missenden High Street in late 2011, as part of a painstaking conservation project, which took almost six months. This most private, creative space – the birthplace of all Roald Dahl's wonderful children's stories – became accessible to the public for the first time.

THERE'S MORE TO ROALD DAHL
THAN GREAT STORIES . . .

Did you know that 10% of author royalties* from this book go to help the work of the Roald Dahl charities?

Roald Dahl is famous for his stories and rhymes, but much less well known is how often he went out of his way to help seriously ill children. Today **Roald Dahl's Marvellous Children's Charity** helps children with the severest conditions and the greatest needs. The charity believes every child can have a more marvellous life, no matter how ill they are, or how short their life may be.

Can you do something marvellous to help others? Find out how at **www.roalddahlcharity.org**

You can find out about Roald Dahl's real-life experiences and how they found their way into his stories at the **Roald Dahl Museum and Story Centre** in Great Missenden, Buckinghamshire (the author's home village). The Museum is a charity that aims to inspire excitement about reading, writing and creativity. There are three fun and fact-packed galleries, with lots to make, do and see (including Roald Dahl's writing hut). Aimed at 6–12-year-olds, the Museum is open to the public and to school groups throughout the year.

Find out more at **www.roalddahlmuseum.org**

WAGGLE YOUR EARS

Or, as the BFG would say, *swiggle* your ears and listen to your favourite Roald Dahl story in your room, in the car, on your way to school or the zoo or to buy chocolate . . .

Listen and laugh as **top-name actors**, including **Stephen Fry**, **Hugh Laurie**, **David Walliams** and **Douglas Hodge**, bring your best-loved Roald Dahl moments to life.

Available on Puffin Audio

Scan the code for PHIZZ-WHIZZING audio clips!

ROALD DAHL'S

Puffin Passport

Autograph	*Roald Dahl*
Birthday	13 September, 1916
Colour of eyes	Blue-grey
Colour of hair	Greyish
Special virtue	Never satisfied with what I've done.
Special vice	Drinking
Favourite colour	Yellow
Favourite food	Caviar

Favourite music   Beethoven

Favourite personality   My wife and children

Favourite sound   Piano

Favourite TV programme   News

Favourite smell   Bacon frying

Favourite book when young   "Mr. Midshipman Easy"

If I wasn't an author I'd like to be   A doctor

My most frightening moment   In a Hurricane, 1941, RAF

My funniest moment   Being born

Motto

My candle burns at both ends
It will not last the night
But ah my foes and oh my friends
It gives a lovely light.

A Day in the Life of

DAHL

Roald Dahl had a very strict daily routine. He would eat breakfast in bed and open his post. At 10.30 a.m. he would walk through the garden to his writing hut and work until 12 p.m. when he went back to the house for lunch – typically, a gin and tonic followed by Norwegian prawns with mayonnaise and lettuce. At the end of every meal, Roald and his family had a chocolate bar chosen from a red plastic box.

After a snooze, he would take a flask of tea back to the writing hut and work from 4 p.m. till 6 p.m. He would be back at the house at exactly six o'clock, ready for his dinner.

He always wrote in pencil and only ever used a very particular kind of yellow pencil with a rubber on the end. Before he started writing, Roald made sure he had six sharpened pencils in a jar by his side. They lasted for two hours before needing to be resharpened.

Roald was *very* particular about the kind of paper he used as well. He wrote all of his books on American yellow legal pads, which were sent to him from New York. He wrote and rewrote until he was sure that every word was just right. A lot of yellow paper was thrown away. Once a month, when his large wastepaper basket was full to overflowing, he made a bonfire just outside his writing hut (where one of the white walls was soon streaked with black soot).

Once Roald had finished writing a book, he gave the pile of yellow scribbled paper to Wendy, his secretary, and she turned it into a neat printed manuscript to send to his publisher.

ROALD DAHL'S
SCHOOL REPORTS

In 1929, when he was thirteen, Roald Dahl was sent to boarding school. You would expect him to get wonderful marks in English – but his school reports were *not* good!

SUMMER TERM, 1930 (aged 14).
English Composition.
'I have never met a boy who so persistently writes the exact opposite of what he means. He seems incapable of marshalling his thoughts on paper.'

His end-of-term reports from this school are of some interest. Here are just four of them, copied word for word from the original documents:

EASTER TERM, 1931 (aged 15). *English Composition.*
'A persistent muddler. Vocabulary negligible, sentences malconstructed. He reminds me of a camel.'

SUMMER TERM, 1932 (aged 16). *English Composition.*
'This boy is an indolent and illiterate member of the class.'

AUTUMN TERM, 1932 (aged 17). *English Composition.*
'Consistently idle. Ideas limited.'

'Little wonder that it never entered my head to become a writer in those days.'

Find out more about Roald Dahl at school in *Boy*.

ROALD DAHL'S
Favourite Things

There is a table in the writing hut on which Roald Dahl kept his collection of special things. And they're all still there.

bottle of shavings from Roald's spine

ball of silver foil – every day, during his time working in London, Roald squashed the wrappers of his Cadbury's Dairy Milk bar and gradually formed this ball; it weighs 310g

Hurricane model plane given to him by his secretary, Wendy

…de rock …taining …e-veined …te

… of …ld's …ur – … is the … joint … …ld's hip

electric pencil sharpener for his special yellow pencils

metal hip joint

school clothes brush – Roald used this to clean his writing board every day

ceramic aspirin paperweight given to Roald by his second wife, Liccy, as a birthday present – it was a joke because she had accused him of behaving like a pill (meaning he was being grumpy)

Take a tour of Roald Dahl's
scrumdiddlyumptious
official website with your
favourite characters at

roalddahl.com

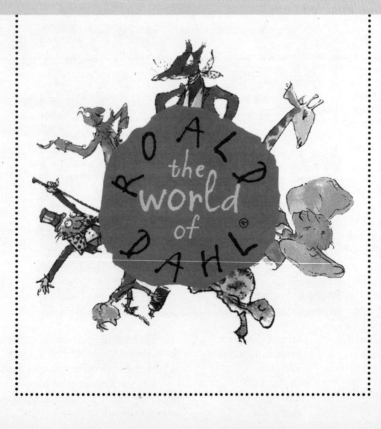